STEVEN RABINOWITZ

Quantity sales special discounts are available on quantity purchases by corporations, associations, and others. For details, contact the publisher at the address above.

Orders by U.S. trade bookstores and wholesalers. Email info@BeyondPublishing.net

The Beyond Publishing Speakers Bureau can bring authors to your live event. For more information or to book an event contact the Beyond Publishing Speakers Bureau speak@BeyondPublishing.net

The Author can be reached directly at BeyondPublishing.net

Manufactured and printed in the United States of America distributed globally by BeyondPublishing.net

BEYOND
PUBLISHING

New York | Los Angeles | London | Sydney

ISBN Hardcover: 978-1-637920-04-6

Wake up...Wake up!!

Gertie...Gertie!!

Can you smell them?

Today is Julie's fifth birthday. Her Mom and Dad were busy setting up the snack table outside before the other children arrive.

Gertie was sleeping under the kitchen table, and Spot noticed a big plate of Donuts outside. Spot yelled again...Gertie, wake up!!! Do you smell them? Can you smell them?

Gertie jumped up and listened to the brown spots on her ear barking to her.

Do you smell them...can you smell them Spot repeated?

Gertie wiggled her nose and breathed in deeply. Yes, I can smell the donuts she growled. I can smell them!!! Sprinkled donuts were Gertie's favorite snack.

I smell donuts Gertie howled. I smell donuts, I need to find those donuts.

Gertie never actually ate a donut. Yet every time Julie had one, rainbow sprinkles always fell to the floor.

Gertie was quick to lick them up and swallow them down. This always gave her a strong burst of energy and super-powers.

Gertie loved the taste of rainbow sprinkles. But this time she wanted to sink her teeth into the entire confection.

How are we going to get to the donuts asked Spot?

That's easy Gertie replied!

Go through the SCARY screen door...

Onto the DARK deck...

Down the SLIPPERY stairs...

Across the long GREEN grass...

And there they are, on the TALL table...

Julie saw that her friend Maggie had arrived and was already playing on the swings in the backyard.

Julie burst through the SCARY screen door. Skated across the DARK deck. Tripped down the SLIPPERY stairs. Ran across the long GREEN grass, around the TALL table, and greeted her friend with a great big smile.

The SCARY screen door was slowly and loudly screeching shut. This is our chance to get outside screamed Spot!

Gertie has always been afraid of the loud and SCARY screen door. She knew this was her only opportunity to get outside if she wanted to get onto the deck, down the stairs, across the grass and to the TALL table with donuts.

Gertie hopped to her paws and as fast as she could, sailed through the screen door and slid onto the DARK deck. The screen door slammed shut behind her with a crashing BIG BOOM!!!

Julie and Maggie were playing on the swings as more children arrived for the party. Nobody even noticed that Gertie had escaped through the screen door.

The DARK deck was old, and the wood had long, sharp splinters that sometimes poked into Gertie's paw. She very slowly crawled across the creaking deck and approached the SLIPPERY stairs.

Julie and her friends were now standing around the snack table. They were laughing and eating the sweet treats that her Mom and Dad had placed on the TALL table.

Spot shouted to Gertie, "we have to hurry if we are going to get down the SLIPPERY stairs, across the long GREEN grass, and to the TALL table before the donuts are all gone!"

The deck stairs were not only SLIPPERY, they were also very steep. Gertie was terrified, but willing to take the leap.

Hurry whimpered Spot!!! If we are going to get a donut, we need to act quickly. Gertie wasted no more time and put her two front paws on the first step of the SLIPPERY stairs.

That's all it took! Gertie lost her balance. She stumbled and tumbled down all four stairs until she lay at the bottom in the long GREEN grass.

Gertie grinned! She hopped to her paws, and immediately dashed right past her Dad who was hanging a candy filled piñata from a tree limb.

"Stop!" he cried out.

"You shouldn't be out of the house" Gertie's Dad roared.

But Gertie raced on heading towards the TALL table with the delicious donuts. Her Dad chased closely behind.

Gertie's Mom was busy putting Julie's birthday presents on the brown bench. From the corner of her eye she noticed Gertie rushing past her.

"Stop!!" she cried out.

"You shouldn't be out of the house" Gertie's Mom hollered.

Gertie continued as fast her paws could carry her. She ran through the long GREEN grass towards the TALL table with donuts. Her Mom chased closely behind.

Julie and Maggie saw Gertie charging towards the TALL table with donuts. They dropped the ball they were tossing and chased after her.

They were both too slow. Gertie had already reached the TALL table with donuts before anybody could stop her.

Spot cried out, "Look, there are rainbow sprinkles in the grass! If you eat the sprinkles, you will get a strong burst of energy and super-powers. You need this to reach the delicious donuts on the TALL table."

Without delay, Gertie gobbled up the sprinkles that fell to the ground.

The rainbow sprinkles were exactly what Gertie needed! This gave her the extra energy and super-powers to jump up and knock the plate of delicious donuts to the ground.

Gertie grabbed a donut in her mouth. She turned around and rushed as rapidly as she could back around the TALL table. She ran through the long GREEN grass and up the SLIPPERY stairs. Now on the DARK deck, she burst through the SCARY screen door, and back under the kitchen table.

Resting in her bed, and out of breath, Gertie gulped down the delicious donut before her Mom and Dad reached her.

Spot whispered to Gertie, "it's time to sleep now, we need to get ready for the next adventure!"

CPSIA information can be obtained
at www.ICGtesting.com
Printed in the USA
BVHW091226090321
602113BV00019B/1964